ANTS
Another Nice Tasty Sweet

Story by R. Watier

Illustrations by M. Watier

"Go to see the ant you lazy one study its ways and learn."

Published by:
MAHRWOOD PRESS Ltd.
31 Zevin Street Suite 8
Jerusalem 97450
ISRAEL

Distributed in the US by:
FELDHEIM PUBLISHERS
208 Airport Executive Park
Nanuet, N.Y. 10954

Printed in Israel

1 2 3 4 5 6 7 8 9 10

*I want to thank my family (blood and otherwise) for helping me reach my dream. They always believed in me, and always said, **"I will listen to you"** when I was working on my books.*

The Sages on learning from the ants

"I observed and took it to heart I saw it and learned a lesson." Thus said the sages of blessed memory; "What did he see? He saw the smallest of all creations and he learned from it a lesson." "What is the smallest of all creations? The Ant" "As it says; go to see the ant you lazy one study its ways and learn. Without leaders officers or rulers, it lays up its stores during the summer and gathers in its food at the harvest."

(Proverbs 24:32) (Proverbs 6:6-8)

In the little town of Gardiner there is a footpath; a footpath that winds between all the houses where all the families and all the children live; a footpath that winds its way past the playground; a footpath which leads to the village center, where you can find the post office, the bank, the book store, the grocery store, and...the bakery.

 O ur story begins on that footpath, where one of the town mothers was walking on her way home from a trip to the bakery, where she had filled her sack with tasty treats for her family. As she walked, one of the giant sweet rolls, the one covered with white, sticky, sugary glaze, fell from her shopping bag.

Down fell the sweet roll, down, down, down to the earth. It hit the path with a THUD, splattering glaze all over everything.

*T*hen the roll, true to its name, rolled off the path, and out of sight, coming to rest under a small green bush. Hidden by leaves and sheltered by shade, the sweet roll disappeared from sight, lost in a different world. The sweet roll landed in a world of roots and leaves; a world unseen by human eyes; a world of...ants.

ou see, there is not one path, but two. Every day, when humans go shopping, so do the ants. If you look closely, there is one path for the humans and another path for the ants.

Have you ever seen ants out shopping? They are very much like us, you know. We get into our cars and make long lines to go to get what we need. And ants do the same; they make long lines, only ants don't have cars.

*I*t is very dangerous for an ant footpath to cross a human footpath, so most ant paths come close to human paths, but few cross them. At about the same time the mother was walking home along the human path, the ants were on their way home from shopping along their path.

Suddenly there was a great wind, and the sky became darker, and darker, and darker still. The ants looked up and saw that the sky was falling.

*T*hen there was a noise, as something came closer, and closer, and closer to earth. The sound started as a soft whistle, but it soon became a deafening screech. Then, suddenly, "SLAM!" the ground shook so hard, that the ants were knocked off of all of their feet.

 And then, "BOOM!" the roll bounced again, and the terrified ants ran in every direction. And then, "SPLAT!" the roll came to rest. In the next instant the ants were being hit by great gobs of white sticky sugar glaze "Plop! Plop! Plop! "

A little girl ant, whose name was Jules, turned and ran straight into the giant sweet roll, hitting it so hard that her face and antennae stuck fast, so that she could barely touch the ground. All the ants wondered what on earth had happened.

They picked themselves up, brushed themselves off, and looked around. They discovered the giant sweet roll resting against the small green bush. All the ants, young and old, were very excited to see this much food in one place. "Why," cried the ants, "this is enough food to feed the whole village all winter!"

"*B*ut how can we move such a cumbersome thing?" cried an ant. So the ants began thinking of how to get the giant sweet roll back to their village. And little Jules, who had freed herself from the sweet roll, thought to herself, "How can I help?"

"How can we move such a large, heavy object?" asked one ant to another. Little Jules said, "I can help!" But no one paid any attention to her, for she was so small, and "What could she know?"

*O*ne thing they did know, was that they had to be quick, for, when the sun was high in the sky, an old man and his

dog, Huff-Huff the Bloodhound, would come down the path.

Nothing, but nothing, but nothing, escaped Huff-Huff's nose, and that would be the end of the giant sweet roll.

 **F**irst they all tried to push on the giant sweet roll, and it rolled a short way.

 *B*ut, suddenly, "BUMP!" it bounced to a halt. It came to rest, flat on the ground, up against a great old log.

The log was so t-a-l-l, and so l-o-n-g, and so w-i-d-e; that the ants could not possibly hope to move the giant sweet roll over it, or around it, to get beyond it, before Huff-Huff came by. And nothing, but nothing, but nothing, escaped his nose.

*W*hat could they do? What could they do? What could they do? Their anthill was only a short distance beyond the old log. They thought, and they thought, and they thought, oh so hard. The task seemed impossible!

And once again, little Jules said, "I can help!" But no one paid any attention to her, for she was so small, and "What could she know?"

 **A**nd so, the ants sat, and the time grew quite short. The ants sat worrying, and fretting, and vainly shoving the Roll, which was wedged tightly against the log and would roll no further.

A third time little Jules said, "I can help!" This time her Grandfather and Grandmother, who had sat alongside the sweet roll to think, turned to little Jules and said, "Tell me, Little One, how can you help?"

And when they heard her idea, they thought it so wise, that they set little Jules on the top of the roll so that she could tell all the others.

"I can cut off a piece of the sweet roll," said Jules to the ants, "a piece just big enough for me to carry over the log. That would help, wouldn't it?" "Yes, that would help." said an ant in the crowd. "But that would make the sweet roll only one tiny piece lighter. Such a tiny amount hardly helps us at all."

"But," said Jules, her voice getting bolder, "if each one of us took what he or she could carry, our job would be finished in no time at all. The roll would be safe in our home before Huff- Huff comes by."

So each ant took a piece of the giant sweet roll, and they formed a long line, and the ants carried the roll, bit by bit, up over the log, along the forest floor, and down into the ant hill.

And when Huff-Huff came puffing along on his leash, he found nothing but crumbs and a brief whiff of frosting, because nothing, but nothing, but nothing escaped his nose.

So the next time you say "I can help," I will listen to you, Little One.

Lessons to be learned from the ant according to the Sages

And said our sages of blessed memory in the Agadata; "Three floors has an ant home. It doesn't put its food not in the bottom floor nor in the top floor, but rather in the middle floor. Not in the top floor because of leaking water (rain, dew,etc) not in the bottom floor because of seeping moisture. Rather they put it in the middle floor.: It only stays alive for six months and it only needs to live on a kernel and a half of wheat, However she goes and brings in the entire summer everything that she finds – wheat, barley, lentils, etc. And if she lives for six months why does she bring in so much? Because she says maybe Hakodosh Baruch Hu will decree more life for me and I will have what to eat. There was a story that they found three hundred measures were gathered by an ant in the ant hill. *(Dvarim Rabbah 5:2)*

What does study its ways and learn mean? Said our sages; see its conduct that it runs away from theft. There was a story with one ant that dropped one kernel of wheat and all the other ants would come and smell it and not one of them would take it. Only the one ant to whom it belonged came eventually and took it.
See what wisdom the ant has that all the other ants just by smelling the kernel knew that it belonged to someone and did not take it, and all this praise the ant did not learn from any other creature therefore it says study its ways and learn. *(Dvarim Rabbah 5:2)*
Maalot hamiddot – Rabbeinu Yechiel ben r' Yekusiel ben r' Binyamin the rofeh

About the author:

M. Watier was born and raised in Maine. He started doodling in his math notebook when he was in third grade. Not because he didn't like math, but because he was good at it and he needed to do something else while he was waiting for his classmates to finish their work.

It was during that crucial part of his life when he received his first complement. And from that moment on he stopped dreaming of being an astronaut or a fireman and dreamt of being an artist.

He is overjoyed that his first book is the collaborative piece that he did with his father.

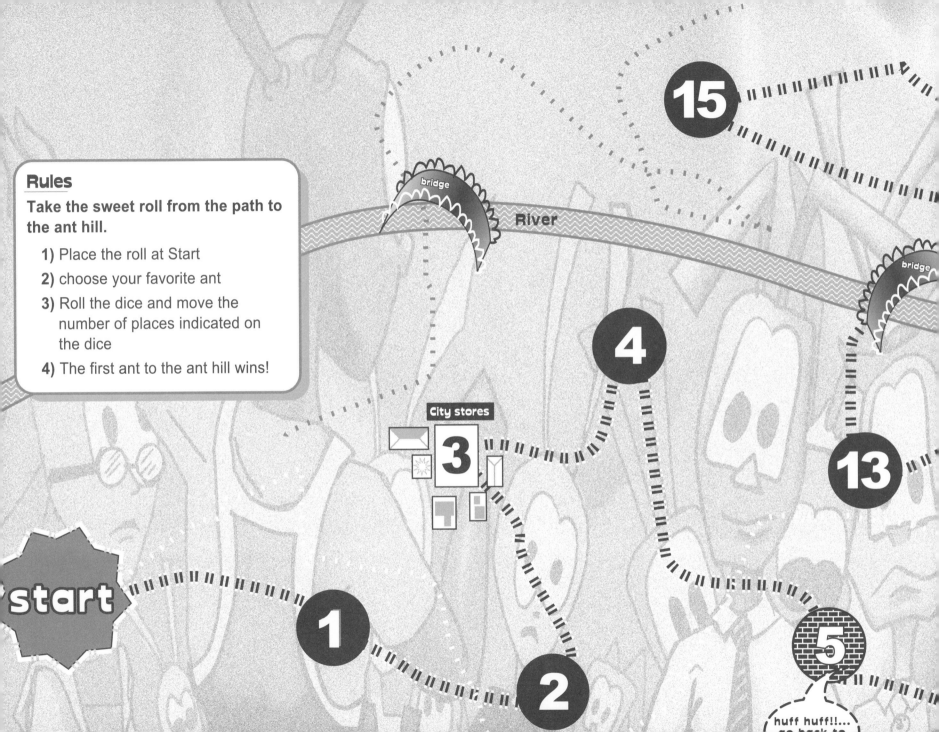